禾 grain hé *(huh)*

fire huǒ *(whoa)*

 秋 autumn qiū *(chew)*

田 field tián *(tee'en)*

苗 sprout miáo *(meow)*

Pronunciation of words in parentheses are approximations of Mandarin Chinese.
Xiao Ming's name is pronounced Schow Ming.

In memory of my father, Ming Ching Lee

Henry Holt and Company, LLC, *Publishers since 1866*
115 West 18th Street, New York, New York 10011
www.henryholt.com

Henry Holt is a registered trademark of Henry Holt and Company, LLC
Copyright © 2005 by Huy Voun Lee. All rights reserved.
Distributed in Canada by H. B. Fenn and Company Ltd.

Library of Congress Cataloging-in-Publication Data
Lee, Huy Voun. In the leaves / Huy Voun Lee.—1st ed.
p.   cm.
Summary: On a visit to a farm, Xiao Ming shows his friends the new Chinese
characters he has learned by explaining that the characters are like pictures.
ISBN-13: 978-0-8050-6764-4
ISBN-10: 0-8050-6764-7
[1. Farm life—Fiction. 2. Chinese characters—Fiction. 3. Chinese language—Vocabulary.]
I. Title. PZ7.L51248Ij 2005   [E]—dc22   2004024278
First Edition—2005 / Designed by Donna Mark
The artist used cut-paper collage to create the illustrations for this book.
Printed in China   10 9 8 7 6 5 4 3 2 1

the Leaves

Huy Voun Lee

秋天

Henry Holt and Company · New York

It is a gorgeous autumn morning. The leaves have changed their colors from green to a rainbow of oranges, reds, and yellows.

Xiao Ming is excited. Today, his mom is taking him and his friends to visit a farm.

He can't wait to see the fields of growing grain. Maybe he can show his friends the new Chinese characters he has learned.

"Writing Chinese characters is really fun," Xiao Ming tells his friends. "It is like drawing pictures." He finds a stick and draws in the soft dirt.

Seiji's
farmhouse
♥ ♥ ♥ ♥

禾 "This is the character for *grain*," he says. "Grain has roots that dig into the ground, just like a tree. First, draw a slanted line on top, like a head of ripe grain and then add the character for *tree*."

"That's so neat!" says Timmy. "Show us another one."

火 "All right. This is *fire*." Xiao Ming draws another character in the dirt.

"It looks like a campfire," says William.

"That's the idea. People used to start fires by rubbing two sticks together," Xiao Ming explains.

秋 "Now, when I put the character for *grain* next to the character for *fire*, I have the character for *autumn*," Xiao Ming says.

"What do fire and grain have to do with autumn?" asks Peggy.

"In autumn, farmers harvest the grain that has ripened in the heat of the sun. From dawn to dusk, they work the fields hoping for a big harvest," says Xiao Ming as he draws.

田 "Is that the character for *field*? It looks just like one," says Timmy.

Xiao Ming nods, smiling. His friends understand!

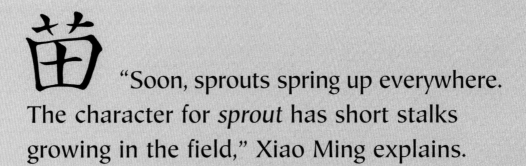

苗 "Soon, sprouts spring up everywhere. The character for *sprout* has short stalks growing in the field," Xiao Ming explains.

豕 He and his friends gather around a pen full of chubby, muddy pigs. "This is the way *pig* was written a long time ago," says Xiao Ming as he draws in the dirt.

"That line is the head and these four lines are the legs. At the end is his curly tail. Is that right, Ming?" Timmy asks.

"Yes!" Xiao Ming cries out. "I was afraid no one would see it."

家 He draws something else. "When I put a pig under a roof, I have the character for *house*. It also means *family*," says Xiao Ming. Everyone looks confused. "The idea is that if there is a pig in the house, there is food for the family."

"That's funny," says William. "What is the next character, Ming?"

口   *"Mouth,"* answers Xiao Ming.
"It's very easy to draw. See, it is a mouth
opening to talk."
    "And ready to eat too!" says Timmy.
"I'm hungry!"
    Everyone laughs.

和 "Just one more character," says Xiao Ming. "Remember the character for *grain*? Put it next to the character for *mouth* and you've made the word for *harmony*. I am always happy to have lots to eat, just like I'm happy to have lots of good friends to eat with. Let's have lunch, Mom!"

米 Xiao Ming and his friends gather around the lunch basket. "You forgot one character," says Xiao Ming's mother. He looks puzzled. "What is your favorite food?" she asks.

"*Rice!*" shouts Xiao Ming and draws the character for his friends.

"I brought some rice balls for lunch," says his mother.

Learning Chinese characters with friends is fun— and so is a picnic!

豕	pig	shǐ	*(ssh'uh)*
家	family	jiā	*(jee'ah)*
口	mouth	kǒu	*(co,* as in *cocoa)*
和	harmony	hé	*(huh)*
米	rice	mǐ	*(mee)*

Pronunciation of words in parentheses are approximations of Mandarin Chinese.